ALL BY MYSELF

BY
MERCER MAYER

A Random House PICTUREBACK® Book

Random House 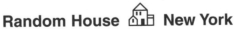 **New York**

All by Myself book, characters, text, and images © 1983 Mercer Mayer. LITTLE CRITTER, MERCER MAYER'S LITTLE CRITTER, and MERCER MAYER'S LITTLE CRITTER and Logo are registered trademarks of Orchard House Licensing Company. All rights reserved. Published in the United States by Random House Children's Books, a division of Random House, Inc., New York. Originally published in 1983 by Golden Books Publishing Company, Inc. PICTUREBACK, RANDOM HOUSE, and the Random House colophon are registered trademarks of Random House, Inc.
www.randomhouse.com/kids
Educators and librarians, for a variety of teaching tools, visit us at
www.randomhouse.com/teachers
Library of Congress Control Number: 82-84108
ISBN-13: 978-0-307-11938-4   ISBN-10: 0-307-11938-6
Printed in the United States of America
50 49 48
First Random House Edition 2006

I can get out of bed
all by myself.

I can button
my overalls.

I can brush my fur.

I can put on my socks…

and tie my shoes.

I can pour some juice
for my little sister…

and help her eat breakfast.

I can pull a duck for her.

I can drive my truck.

I can ride my bike.

I can give a drink
to my bear.

I can kick my ball...

and roll on the ground.

I can pound with
my hammer.

I can sail my boat.

I can look after
my little sister.

I can help Dad
trim a bush…

or ice a cake for Mom.

I can look at a
book and find
a mouse.

I can color a picture.

I can put my toys away...

and get into my pajamas.

I can brush my teeth.

I can put myself to bed...

but I can't go to sleep
without a story.

Good night.